"Choose Your Own Adventure is the best thing that has come along since books themselves."
—Alysha Beyer, age 11

"I didn't read much before, but now I read my Choose Your Own Adventure books almost every night."
—Chris Brogan, age 13

"I love the control I have over what happens next."
—Kosta Efstathiou, age 17

"Choose Your Own Adventure books are so much fun to read and collect—I want them all!"
—Brendan Davin, age 11

And teachers like this series, too:
"We have read and reread, worn thin, loved, loaned, bought for others, and donated to school libraries our Choose Your Own Adventure books."

**CHOOSE YOUR OWN ADVENTURE®—
AND MAKE READING MORE FUN!**

Bantam Books in the Choose Your Own Adventure® series
Ask your bookseller for the books you have missed

MASTER OF TAE KWON DO

BY RICHARD BRIGHTFIELD

ILLUSTRATED BY FRANK BOLLE

An Edward Packard Book

BANTAM BOOKS
NEW YORK • TORONTO • LONDON • SYDNEY • AUCKLAND

RL 4, age 10 and up

MASTER OF TAE KWON DO
A Bantam Book / June 1990

*CHOOSE YOUR OWN ADVENTURE® is a registered trademark of
Bantam Books, a division of Bantam Doubleday Dell Publishing Group,
Inc. Registered in U.S. Patent and Trademark Office and elsewhere.*

Original conception of Edward Packard

*Cover art by David Mattingly
Interior illustrations by Frank Bolle*

ISBN 0-553-28516-2

Published simultaneously in the United States and Canada

PRINTED IN THE UNITED STATES OF AMERICA

OPM   0 9 8 7

For Susan Korman, Charles Kochman, Janaima Cabral, Bruno Klang, and Kim Kyong Nim

WARNING!!!

Do not read this book straight through from beginning to end. These pages contain many different adventures that you may have when you are sent to Korea to study tae kwon do and locate your missing friend. From time to time as you read along, you will be asked to make a choice. Your choice may lead to success or disaster!

The adventures you have are the results of your choices. You are responsible because you choose! After you make a choice, follow the instructions to see what happens to you next.

Think carefully before you make a decision. In your last adventure, *Master of Kung Fu,* you went to China on a kung fu tour. Now, in Korea, you may face many new and unexpected adventures. Even if you become a master of tae kwon do and succeed in finding your friend, you may discover that the goal of your mission is no longer the same!

Good luck!

The school bus rumbles down the street. With safety lights flashing, it comes to a stop at the corner near your house. You jump off and start up the block.

As you get closer to your house, you notice a large, official-looking car parked out front. Two men in dark business suits are standing next to it. One of them sees you coming and nudges the smaller man next to him with his elbow. They start toward you.

At the same moment, your mother comes running out of the front door.

"They want to ask you some questions!" she calls over. "But come into the house first."

You make a wide detour around the car and run up the steps to the front porch. Whoever these men are, you think, they look like bad news.

Inside the house, your mother sits down on the edge of the sofa, looking nervous. The two men stand by the window. From time to time the shorter one peers outside, as if he expects someone else to arrive.

"For starters," the tall man says, flipping open a wallet and showing his ID, "let me introduce myself. My name is Jake McKenna, and this is my associate, Arnold Borkin. We're from the CIA, the Central Intelligence Agency. I'm sure you've heard of our organization."

Turn to page 2.

"We know about your trip to China last year and your interest in the martial arts," Borkin continues with a broad smile that looks a bit forced. "We have an offer for you. We've been looking for someone to go to Korea and act as an undercover agent—someone who won't arouse suspicion."

"An agent? What am I supposed to do?" you ask, surprised.

"Well, for one thing, you'll be studying tae kwon do, the Korean form of martial arts—partly as a cover. And while you're there, we want you to keep an eye out for this woman."

Borkin takes out a small photograph from his inside pocket and hands it to you. You look at the picture and almost jump. It's a picture of Ling, the Chinese girl who taught you kung fu when you were in China last year.

"I know her!" you exclaim. "She's—"

"We know," Borkin interrupts. "She is also one of our top agents in the Far East."

"Or was," says McKenna. "We don't know if she's still alive."

"If people are being killed, I certainly don't think you should go," your mother interrupts.

"Think of it as a vital mission for your country," Borkin says. "And besides, you owe it to Ling."

"I still say—" your mother starts.

"There's no danger—or very little," McKenna interrupts. "And it's something of supreme importance to national security."

"What do I do if I find Ling?" you ask.

Go on to the next page.

Borkin hands you a set of instructions:

1. When you reach Seoul, enroll in a tae kwon do school of your choice.
2. Keep a lookout for any information concerning the whereabouts of Ling.
3. If Ling is located, immediately activate the miniature transmitter hidden in your wristwatch by pulling the time-setting knob free from the watch. This will send the proper signal.
4. Do not use the transmitter for any other purpose.

"Burn these instructions as soon as you have them memorized," Borkin says. "Right now you have to decide if you want to go directly to Korea when your summer vacation starts or if you want to get in two weeks of special training in undercover work at our camp in Maryland first."

"I haven't even said I'll go," you point out to the two agents. But deep down you've already decided that you wouldn't miss this for anything.

If you decide to go directly to Korea,
turn to page 57.

If you decide to go to the training camp first,
turn to page 103.

You stare as dozens of paratroopers hit the ground all around the village. One of them landing nearby is not Korean. It's Borkin, the agent from the CIA! He drops his parachute harness and walks over to you.

"We got your signal," he says. "Where is she?"

"Oh, right—the signal! Ling is trying to escape from Kong-yi's men. She's up there on that hill in the distance, I think. You've got to help her. Kong-yi is insane. He thinks he can take over North and South Korea."

Agent Borkin stands there rubbing his chin. "So you know about that, do you," he says with an evil grin. "I think, perhaps, you know too much."

He gives a signal, and several of the soldiers run over and tie your hands behind your back.

"We have a small prison island off the west coast of Korea where you will be our guest for a while."

"How long?" you ask.

He smiles cruelly. "Until we see a passing shark that would like a good meal."

The End

"I'd rather go with you than stay behind," you tell Ling.

One of the local Koreans runs inside with your shoes. You quickly put them on and help Ling gather up her maps and charts. Then the two of you dash out the back door and along a narrow pathway between the flooded rice fields. You slip a couple of times and sink up to your knees in the muddy water before you can climb back onto the path. From the other side of the village, you can hear more firing.

"If we can get to the base of that hill up ahead, we'll be all right," Ling shouts back as she runs ahead of you.

You move as fast as you can. You see splashes on the surface of the rice paddy next to you, followed by sharp rifle cracks from behind.

"Ling, they're firing at us!"

"Don't think about it, just keep going," she calls back.

Finally you reach the base of the hill and plunge into the woods. A trail runs almost directly upward. You stumble up the hill, already out of breath, grasping at the branches on both sides to pull yourself along.

You keep up with Ling as best you can. Finally she stops and sits with her back up against a tree.

"We'll rest for a few moments," she says, "then keep going. Kong-yi's men on the ground won't follow us here, but we have to get over this hill before their backup help arrives from the air."

"Help from the air?"

Turn to page 58.

You settle back in your seat and watch the scenery below as the plane soars up into the sky. An Oriental girl about your age is sitting next to you. She leans over to look out the window.

"Oh, excuse me," she says. "I didn't mean to disturb you."

"You didn't," you say, introducing yourself.

"My name is Joan Pyun. I'm going home to Korea after spending a year studying in your country," she tells you.

"You speak English very well," you say.

"Thank you," Joan says. "My father's company manufactures electronic products. He sells them mostly in the United States. That is why he sent me here to learn your language."

"Your family sounds rich," you say.

"We have been lucky," she says. "My father has told me many stories about what he went through as a young child during the war with the North Koreans. His family was penniless, their home and possessions burned. The Americans kept them from starving. That is why he gave me an American name—to honor them. To this day, the North and South are still divided. We have relatives trapped in the North that I have never seen or heard from."

"The North Koreans sound pretty bad," you say.

"They are not really bad. They are victims of history," Joan says. "They are still Koreans, and we love them. I dream always that one day our country will be reunited."

Turn to page 62.

8

"This is the hotel," Joan says. "I must leave you now, but I really enjoyed our conversations. My chauffeur will carry your bags into the hotel and speak to the desk clerk. Here is my father's business card. If you need to, you can get in touch with me through his office."

"I really appreciate all of your help," you say.

"I'm glad we met," she says.

You wave good-bye and follow the chauffeur into the glittering lobby of the hotel. He speaks to the clerk and hands him a small envelope. A bellboy takes your bags and leads you to the elevator. You go all the way up to one of the top floors. At the end of a wide, carpeted hallway, the bellboy opens the door to a large suite of rooms. You can hardly believe your eyes.

The suite in front of you looks like the ultimate in luxury. The broad expanse of the living room seems to go on forever until it reaches the floor-to-ceiling windows at the far end. Large overstuffed chairs and sofas covered with soft white leather fill the room.

The bedroom has a king-sized bed. It makes you feel like lying down and taking a nap. In fact, you are weary after your long flight. On the other hand, you've just arrived in an exciting new city on the other side of the world—a city you can't wait to explore.

If you decide to take a nap first,
turn to page 42.

If you decide to go out and explore the city,
turn to page 53.

You decide to take Pak's advice. You've been thinking along the same lines yourself since the attack outside in the street. Also, you don't want to be caught in the middle between the CIA and Ling, or whatever she's involved with now.

"Go back to the main street and take a cab," Pak says. "No one will try to stop you. It's me they're after. I'll wait here awhile longer."

You thank Pak and go back through the tunnel and up the stairway to the outside. You dash down the dark street. By the time you reach the busy intersection, you are out of breath.

Back at the hotel, you tell the desk clerk that you are checking out. The clerk looks both surprised and nervous!

"Checking out?" he says. "You are not enjoying yourself here?"

"It's not that," you say. "It's just—"

Before you can finish your sentence, the clerk runs over to the far corner behind the counter and starts making a telephone call. You take the elevator up to your suite.

Turn to page 66.

At the bottom of the stairs, you stop for a moment. The noise is much louder now and coming from the other side of a green curtain. You take a deep breath, push the curtain aside, and step into a large, dimly lit room with a vaulted ceiling.

There is a bar along one side and a dozen round tables on the floor of the restaurant. You don't see any food being served, but there are lots of drinks on the tables.

The noise dims somewhat as you enter, and several of the rough-looking patrons stop what they're doing and turn to look in your direction. A slim Japanese man sitting alone at a table in the far corner motions for you to come over.

You thread your way among the tables, careful not to bump into anyone. You sit down next to the man who called you over.

"You got my note, I see. I'm glad you came. My name Kenzo Ohki. Represent Japanese Yakuza. Wish to make a deal," he says.

"*Yakuza?* What is that?" you ask.

"Yakuza are businessmen. Trade in delicate areas."

"In other words, you're gangsters," you say.

"Term *gangster* not accurate. But some would consider us that."

"What's the deal?" you ask.

Turn to page 20.

12

"Maybe later," you say. "Right now, I'm going to go back to my hotel and get some sleep."

"Here is the address," Pak Sik says, handing you a card. One side is printed in Korean, the other side in English. It says YUM DUK KWAN, 34 Chongno Street, tel. 365–2389.

You thank Pak, who looks genuinely disappointed, and go back to the street, heading toward the hotel.

When you get back to your suite, you unpack your bags. Something is strange, though. You have a habit of always rolling up a pair of socks in a single ball when you pack them. But with one pair, each sock is now rolled up separately. You don't remember doing *that*. Suddenly you realize that someone has searched your things and in haste rolled up your socks differently.

And your picture of Ling, the one that Borkin from the CIA gave you, is gone. You wonder why anyone would want to take it. Nothing else is missing. Thank goodness you carefully burned the list of secret instructions back in the States before you left.

You take a shower in the luxurious bathroom and are about to lie down when the phone by the bed starts ringing. You pick up the receiver.

"Hello?" you say. There is nothing but silence on the other end. You try to get a response a few more times before hanging up, but there's nothing! A wrong number? you wonder.

Turn to page 72.

"What are the other things around it?"

"They are the four trigrams representing the Sun, Moon, Heaven, and Earth, and also the four directions. Each trigram has many philosophical meanings. So you see, our flag is very much like us—very complex. I wish I could talk with you more, but right now I have to go," she says, standing up and glancing over toward the entrance of the restaurant, as if someone were watching her. "And do yourself a favor. Find another school."

She leaves just as they serve you your dinner.

You think about Joan's advice and her reaction when you mentioned the Yum Duk Kwan. Perhaps you should change schools. Then again, maybe Joan was just being overly protective. You'd hate to change schools for nothing.

If you follow Joan's advice and find another tae kwon do school, turn to page 38.

If you stay with the Yum Duk Kwan, turn to page 84.

"I'm going to 34 Chong-no Street," you tell the driver, reading the address off of Pak's card.

"That street very crowded with people this time of night," the driver says. "But I can let you off not too far from where you want to go."

The cab creeps through the streets. It looks like everyone in the city is out for the evening. The driver stops in the middle of the street and points. You pay him and get out of the cab, launching yourself into the crowd.

The school has a large neon sign picturing a tae kwon do fighter giving a flying kick in three stages, each flashing in sequence. Underneath this is a large, arched doorway between two stores. You go up three flights of rickety wooden stairs.

Bloodcurdling shouts are coming from inside. You open the door a crack and peek in. Inside is a large room with a high ceiling. A long row of figures, all dressed in white martial arts costumes with black belts, are seated at one side. A figure is seated on the floor alone in the center. Still another figure is leaping around that one. The moving figure—with a fierce cry—leaps into the air and throws a vicious kick. You'd swear that the foot of the attacker was going to knock the head off the one on the floor, but it stops a fraction of an inch short. The seated figure doesn't move a muscle or even change his expression. He then gets up, bows to the attacker, and joins the row of other figures seated at the side. The attacker says something in Korean, and they all get up and file out another door on the side. Then he comes over to you.

Turn to page 79.

16

You dive after her into a hole in the ground and drop five or six feet onto a thick bed of pine needles. There is just enough light for you to see that a tunnel leads off to the side. Its ceiling is supported by logs.

"This must be a bunker of some sort," Ling says, "built by one side or the other during the war between the North and the South. Most of these hills around here were fortified. It's amazing that it's still in such good shape after 36 years. As long as we're this deep in the ground, there's no way they can spot us from the air."

There is another explosion outside, this time farther away.

"See, they've already lost us," Ling says. "Now we can relax for a while. But before we go on, there is something I must ask you. Will you join us to help defeat Kong-yi and stop him from carrying out his evil plans?"

"If what you say about Kong-yi is true, then I'm with you all the way."

You hope you know what you're getting yourself into. Being a spy for the CIA was bad enough, but working to stop the overthrow of the Korean government! You're not sure what to think anymore.

You wait awhile for the coast to clear. Then you follow Ling into the darkness of the night.

The End

It was probably the Korean girl, Joan Pyun, who paid for your hotel. You'll have to call and thank her later. You wonder why she did it. Is she that generous—or that rich?

You take a cab to the tae kwon do school. It is almost nine-thirty. There is a bus already parked in front. It reminds you of the one you took on your kung fu tour of China last year. The other students are lined up, ready to get on. They are a tough-looking bunch. You wonder for a moment what you are getting yourself into. You almost decide to forget the whole thing and go back to the hotel. But you didn't come all the way over here just to turn around and chicken out.

You get on the bus with the others and take a seat near the front. Shin Chung gets in and takes the seat next to you.

"I'm glad you decided to study with us," he says. "We are like a large family." Then he turns and starts reading a book in Korean.

The bus pulls away from the curb and heads out of the city. Soon it is through the suburbs and on a superhighway heading east. For the next couple of hours, the bus speeds past high, rolling hills. In the early afternoon it turns off onto a side road and starts climbing up into the Sorak Mountains.

Suddenly, as he is coming around a curve, the driver sees a heavy log across the road and quickly slams on the brakes. You look out the window and see hooded, black-clad figures spring up from behind the log and from behind rocks on the sides of the road.

Turn to page 25.

"The manager said he saw you come in here," she says. "I was passing by, so I thought I'd see how you were doing."

You invite her to join you.

"Thanks," she says. "But I can only stay for a few minutes."

"I've enrolled already for tae kwon do classes at something called the Yum Duk Kwan," you tell Joan.

For a moment Joan's smooth, ivory-colored skin seems to get a shade paler, and the pupils of her almond-shaped eyes open wide.

"You've heard of that school?" you ask.

"No . . . not really," she says. But there is something in the way she says it that indicates that she's not telling you something.

"Maybe I should find a different school," you say. "I don't really know anything about this one."

"I . . . I think you should," she says. "Yes, now I remember. The school you mentioned does not have a good reputation. There are many other tae kwon do schools in Seoul that would be better."

"I've only been here for a little while, so it may not be fair for me to say this, but I find the Koreans hard to figure out," you say, changing the subject.

"That's true. We are a people of many contradictions," Joan says. "We are like the symbol on our flag. Here is a picture of it on the cover of the menu. The circle in the middle divided in half by an S-curve, what we call the *Taeguk*, is like the Chinese yin-yang symbol—half light, half dark, positive and negative, but constantly interacting."

Turn to page 13.

Kenzo takes out a small photo and places it on the table. It's the picture of Ling that Borkin gave you.

"That's mine!" you exclaim. "You're the one who must have stolen it from my room!"

"Whatever," Kenzo says calmly. "Need information about this person. We hire her as agent. She spy on Triads in Seoul Chinatown. Is she double agent? Need you to find out."

Kenzo suddenly stares across the room, a look of surprise on his face. Three men have come into the restaurant. You can't tell if they are Chinese or Korean. They look mean, that much you do know.

The door to the kitchen is behind the bar. Kenzo makes a brief gesture for you to follow him and then makes a run for it.

You're not sure who Kenzo is, or what the Yakuza are all about. It might be best to just stay where you are and get away from Kenzo. Then again, those men do not look very friendly. And in the long run, Kenzo might be able to help you.

If you follow Kenzo, turn to page 117.

If you stay where you are, turn to page 75.

"I'll go to the mountains," you say.

"Very good," Chung says. "We have a bus leaving from here tomorrow morning at nine-thirty."

You thank Chung and go back down the stairway to the street. You remember the note you got at the hotel and take it out. As far as you can make out, it tells you to go to the White Crane restaurant on Taep Street. You decide to go there on the way back to your hotel.

You look at a map and go down to the subway. A train is coming into the station as you pay your fare and walk onto the platform. You get in the first car and ride five stops.

When you come out of the subway, the street is almost deserted and much darker than in the other part of town. There are no signposts or street names—not that you could read them in Korean, anyway.

Off the main thoroughfare, the streets deterio rate into a maze of narrow alleys. You are exploring down one of them when a police car and an ambulance, lights flashing but without sirens, come tearing down the street. You press yourself against a concrete wall as they go speeding by.

The cars screech to a halt at the end of the block. You carefully walk closer to see what's going on. You notice a small sign just above the doorway where the cars are parked. It has a picture of a white crane.

Turn to page 71.

Pyun's office is gigantic, with a white marble floor, walls paneled in dark wood, and a latticed ceiling at least fifteen feet high. At the far end, covering the wall from floor to ceiling, is a map of the world. It is designed so that Korea itself is at the exact center, highlighted in gold.

A Korean man, barely five feet tall and dressed in a Western business suit, comes out from behind a low but oversized desk and points to the map. "Today Korea, tomorrow the world," he says.

"I came here to see your daughter," you say.

"Joan is out of the country at the moment," Pyun says.

"But her driver said—"

"Ah, yes. I guess he was confused. In any event, I had him bring you here so that I could offer you a proposition. I have sources that say you are a spy for the American CIA. I don't want to interfere with that. In fact, I want you to succeed in finding this . . . Ling woman. What I *also* want is for you to get a regular job with the CIA after you return to America. Then I just want you to find out how much they know about my operations and report to me at your convenience. It may take you a while to do all this, but I am patient—up to a point. If you are successful, you will be greatly rewarded."

Is this man on the level? you wonder. His offer sounds easy enough, and the prospect of being greatly rewarded sounds inviting. But can you trust him?

If you accept Pyun's proposal, turn to page 36.

If you refuse, turn to page 82.

You go back to the main street and walk, looking for a cab to take you back to your hotel. The sooner you get out of this neighborhood the better, you feel. You can sense danger all around you. When you get to another, busier intersection, you are relieved to find a taxi.

When you are back in your room, you pick up the phone and ask room service to send up something to eat.

Ten minutes later there is a knock at the door. A porter brings in a black lacquer tray with several small metal bowls filled with food, a knife and a fork, chopsticks, and a soupspoon. He puts the tray down on a large glass coffee table in front of one of the overstuffed sofas. You tip the porter but stop him before he gets to the door.

"Do you speak English?" you ask.

"Some English. Many guests in hotel speak only English."

"Maybe you can help me out," you say. " I have these words. I'd like to know what they mean."

You show the porter the lettering on the back of Ling's picture. When he sees it, a shocked expression covers his face, almost one of horror.

"That . . . that mean Red Dragon Society," he stammers. "It's written in Chinese. Wha . . . why you have that?"

"Red Dragon?"

"Red Dragon is Chinese. From Hong Kong and Macao. Very bad name. What Chinese call *Triad*—gangsters, killers. Do very bad things, even here in Seoul."

Turn to page 28.

"Are those Ninja?" you ask Chung, but he is out the front door of the bus before you can finish the question. The rest of the tae kwon do fighters stream out behind him.

As you jump off the bus and take cover behind some rocks, you see the black-suited figures flying through the air, directing vicious kicks at the students from the bus.

Soon most of the students are down. They don't seem to be a match for the attackers. Except for Chung. You watch in amazement as he leaps into the air and fells several enemies with incredible flying kicks.

Then you hear a sharp crack from a nearby hillside. Chung is knocked backward to the ground by what must have been a rifle shot. His right shoulder has been hit, staining the front of his white tunic bright red.

Two of the remaining tae kwon do students are pulling Chung to the cover of some boulders next to the road when the bus erupts with a terrific explosion—throwing flaming debris all over the place.

A piece hits you in the head, and suddenly everything goes black.

Turn to page 56.

You find a pencil and write down the name and address above the Japanese writing in the notebook, so you won't forget it. Then you go out of the restaurant and walk back to the subway. There's no use trying to find a cab in this neighborhood. You take the subway five stops back to where you got on earlier and find a cabdriver there who can speak English.

"Ah, you wish to gamble," the driver says when he hears the address. "I take many people there. That Tai-Sai Casino. Very fancy."

"Is it by any chance run by Japanese?" you ask.

"Japanese not popular around here for long time after world war. Now some come back, invest money quietly in ventures. I think casino is one of them."

A half mile before you get to the casino, limousines are parked bumper-to-bumper, the drivers still waiting inside the cars. Up ahead, you see the tall neon sign with flashing Korean characters. At the bottom of the sign, in smaller lettering, are the words TAI-SAI CASINO.

As you pay the cabdriver, a bow-tied doorman comes over and opens the car door for you. All smiles, he also opens the door of the casino as you go in.

Inside, the floor of the cavernous hall is filled with gambling tables. You recognize roulette, poker, blackjack, and dice being played.

Go on to the next page.

The tables are surrounded by men and women, most of whom are in formal dress, though some of the men are wearing business suits. Enormous crystal chandeliers hang from the high ceiling.

A man in a tuxedo comes over and says something to you in Korean.

"I'm sorry," you say. "I don't speak your language."

"Oh, you American?" he says, bowing slightly as he speaks. "Many welcomes. You wish to play at tables?"

"Actually, I'm here looking for a man named Kenzo Ohki. He's Japanese."

"Kenzo?" he says. "You better speak with manager."

Turn to page 81.

"Thanks for telling me, and . . ." But the porter is already through the door of your suite and running down the hall toward the elevator.

You close the door, lock it from the inside, and walk back to the coffee table. You try the food. It tastes very good, even if you don't know what it is.

Red Dragon, you think. The porter certainly seemed concerned. Gangsters, he said. You can only wonder about its meaning.

Your body is still many hours behind and trying to catch up with your new time schedule. You're not really tired, especially since you slept all day. But you still feel groggy.

In one corner of the living room is a very large TV screen. You turn it on and watch a rerun of "Magnum, P.I." dubbed in Korean. Then you watch several local shows and finally fall asleep in one of the overstuffed chairs.

Early light streaming through the high windows wakes you up. You go over to them and look out over the city glittering in the morning sun.

You take a bath in the enormous bathtub, then change your clothes and pack your bags.

You take a last look at the luxurious suite, sigh, and carrying your own bags, take the elevator down to the front desk.

"How much do I owe?" you ask the clerk.

"Everything has been taken care of," he says.

"Taken care of? By whom?"

"I'm not at liberty to say. I hope you enjoyed your visit," the clerk says, turning away to help someone else.

Turn to page 17.

You study tae kwon do every day with Toku. At the end of two weeks, you have an idea what the basic forms are as well as having learned some of the more spectacular kicks that tae kwon do specializes in. Still you realize that you have a lot more to learn.

You are then called into McFee's office. "This woman, Ling, seems to have contacts all over the place, particularly in Korea and Japan," he says. "In Japan she has connections with the Yakuza. The Yakuza are referred to as the Japanese Mafia, although in many ways they are different. But you need not worry. As far as your search for her is concerned, I suggest you start in either Korea or Japan."

Either choice, at this point, seems as good as the other. But you must make your decision now.

If you decide to search in Korea, turn to page 116.

If you decide to search in Japan, turn to page 74.

The light inside the house is dim, but you recognize Ling immediately. She looks up and smiles.

"I'm certainly glad to see you," you say. "Borkin and McKenna told me you might be dead."

"The agents you speak about would certainly *like* to kill me," she says. "I imagine you were sent to track me down so that they could do just that."

"But don't you work for them too?"

"Borkin and McKenna are what we call 'moles' who have burrowed into the American CIA. They see Kong-yi as the best hope for South Korea taking over North Korea. And he has promised them that they will share his power. He's yet another would-be tyrant with delusions of grandeur. Everyone would like to see the unification of Korea, but Kong-yi only wants to become ruler and dictator."

"What should I do?" you ask. "I'm supposed to send a signal when I find you."

"We must decide how to—" Ling starts, but she is cut short as Wu Bai bursts into the room. He tells her something in rapid Chinese.

"We are under attack by Kong-yi's men," Ling says. "We are outnumbered, and there is no way to fight bullets even if one knows martial arts. I must go deeper into the mountains. You can either come with me or stay here. My Korean friends in the village will hide you if you want."

There's no telling what will happen to you no matter what you choose. Either way, whatever your decision, you have to make it fast.

If you go with Ling, turn to page 5.

If you hide in the village, turn to page 59.

32

Your Korean friend leads you through the village to one of the houses. You follow his example and take off your shoes before entering.

Inside, several of the students from the bus are lying on thin cotton mattresses spread around the floor. One of them is Chung.

"I'm glad to see that you are all right," he says.

"I'm glad you are, too," you say with relief.

"I'll be up and around in a few days. Right now, the village *mudangs,* the women shamans, or faith healers as you might call them in your country, say that I need rest. Some of the others are well enough to travel, although the trails are still dangerous. Enemies are stalking us."

"Who are these enemies?" you ask. "I thought we were just going to a tae kwon do school."

"We are also fighters with a righteous cause. There are those who wish to stop us. But that will be explained to you in time. Right now you should decide if you want to continue on to the school despite the dangers, or return to Seoul."

You've been given the opportunity to leave. Perhaps you should take advantage of it and go home. It's a little more dangerous than you expected. On the other hand, you were sent to Korea to locate Ling. If you stay with the school, you might find her.

If you continue on to the school,
turn to page 100.

If you decide to go back to Seoul,
turn to page 89.

Why was the monk so cautious? you wonder. Then you realize the room must be bugged. Now you're sure this place is not on the up-and-up. You sit there, trying to figure out what to do.

Right now, you might as well try the vegetables. They turn out to be very hot—hot as in spicy. You add a little—very little—to the rice and eat it. It doesn't taste bad at all.

The room has regular electric lights, and you turn on the desk lamp as it gets dark outside. You look around the room, almost expecting to find a TV set, but no such luck. The only thing you find are several books in one of the desk drawers, but they are all in Korean.

You turn off the light, lie down on the bed, and drift off to sleep, thinking about the monk's warning.

Later, you wake up in the dark, realizing that someone is in the room. A hand is suddenly clamped over your mouth.

"Don't cry out," a low voice whispers in your ear "I am here to help you escape."

You recognize at once the monk who brought you the food earlier. You realize that you have to decide whether you are going to try to escape right now with his help, or if you are going to wait. Since you don't know who this man is, you could be walking into even more trouble.

If you decide to try to escape now, turn to page 119.

If you decide to wait, turn to page 80.

The two tae kwon do students seem to gain new strength as they move forward up the road. You follow along behind them. After a few miles, they switch to a trail going up through the trees. Your head is still throbbing from the explosion. It doesn't help that you are struggling to keep up with the two students ahead of you.

The trail follows the ridge of the mountains, dipping down every so often. Finally you come over a ridge and see, nestled in a valley below, what looks like a small Buddhist monastery. It is not unlike the ones you saw in China. Strangely, a large, plain, cube-shaped building without windows is halfway up the mountain on the other side.

As you walk down the steep trail leading to the monastery, you see a central courtyard filled with rows of students practicing their tae kwon do exercises in unison.

You follow the two students as they enter the monastery grounds through the main gate. You skirt around the open courtyard and enter a large temple. Inside, the walls are lavishly decorated in green, red, and gold. The gigantic Buddha image at the far side of the otherwise empty hall is unlike any you've seen. Its head is weirdly large in proportion to the rest of its body.

The two students you followed duck into a small door to one side of the Buddha. You are about to follow them when an elderly Korean man dressed in a monk's robe steps through the door and raises his hand in a signal for you to stop.

Turn to page 95.

"I think I can handle it," you say.

"Very good. I'm glad you have accepted," Pyun says, coming over and shaking your hand. "I'll hold you to it. Remember, though, I have operatives worldwide. If you don't fulfill your part of the bargain, well, I don't want to think of what will happen to you."

You finish your tae kwon do training at the Yum Duk Kwan. At the end of the summer you go back home and return to school. Shortly after graduation, you get a letter offering you a job in the CIA.

You are thinking about what to do when the phone rings.

"Hello. This is Joan Pyun," a voice says on the other end. "I'm in the States, in fact, only a few blocks away. I must talk with you right away."

You suddenly realize that your life is about to get very complicated once again.

The End

The group goes outside and across several courtyards, then into a kind of cafeteria building. A monk attendant hands you a bowl and another one fills it with a thin soup. You recognize the monk doling the soup out—he's the one from yesterday who warned you to leave. Your eyes meet for a moment, then you take your bowl and go into a hall where all the other students are eating.

You are just finishing your meal when you see a familiar figure beckoning you from the other side of the hall—it's Chung! Miraculously, he looks completely recovered. You go over and follow him outside.

"Chung, I'm glad—" you begin, but he interrupts.

"I hope you are ready to start your training," he says. "Most of the students are required to do manual work in the morning, but since your time is short . . . I mean, since you're just here for the summer, we'll forget about the work. As soon as you can change into your practice uniform, meet me in the main courtyard."

He leaves before you can ask him how he got to the monastery.

When you get to the courtyard, you see Chung sitting on the ground meditating. When he sees you, he gets to his feet and springs into the air almost in one motion. His foot snaps out and whizzes past your head, so close that you feel the breeze it makes as it goes by.

Turn to page 85.

You decide to follow Joan's advice and find another tae kwon do school, the Chung Moo Kwan. After a week at the Hilton, you find a small but comfortable room in a hotel on the same block as the kwan.

The instructors at Chung Moo are very thorough, and soon you are advancing rapidly.

You don't hear anything more from Shin Chung and the people at the Yum Duk Kwan—or from Joan for that matter. You call her father's office, and they tell you that she is out of the country again.

At the end of the summer, you pack up your bags and head home. When you get back to the States, you try to call Borkin and McKenna, but the CIA operator in Alexandria, Virginia, won't put you through.

You still have the watch they sent you. You figure if you ever do run into Ling again, you can pull out the time-setting knob and send out a signal.

The End

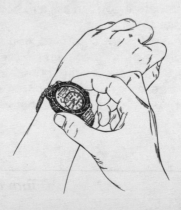

"I'll help you," you tell Ling. "It's the least I can do after all you did for me in China."

Chun-chu hands you a package. "Here is a sul sa do costume," he says. "Put it on—and good luck!"

With that, he steps back and vanishes into the darkness.

You follow Ling across the ridge toward Kong-yi's cube-shaped building.

About a half a mile away, you come to an opening in the ground. A rush of air is going into it.

"This is a ventilation shaft," Ling says. "You stand guard while I go down."

She attaches one end of a rope around a pointed rock that is sticking out of the ground. Then she vanishes down the shaft.

You wait, listening intently. Then you hear what sounds like footsteps crunching on the gravel of the trail not far away. You decide that you have to warn Ling.

Turn to page 61.

Kyo leads you out of the hall, across a small courtyard in the back, and into another building. Then you go down to the end of a long hallway.

"This will be your quarters," Kyo says, opening a door.

The inside of the room is furnished with richly decorated furniture—a large, comfortable-looking bed, a dresser, and a desk and chair. In the back, another door opens into a small bathroom.

"We thought we'd do as much as possible to make you feel comfortable," Kyo says. "You will find fresh clothes in the dresser. We have only two meals a day here, one at dawn and the other just before noon. But since you missed the noon meal today, I'll have some refreshments sent over."

With this, Kyo disappears back down the hall.

You sit there for a while, wondering what you've gotten yourself into, and what kind of monastery this is—if it really is a monastery.

A man in monk's robes carrying a tray with a bowl of rice and one of cooked vegetables appears at the door. He enters the room and places the tray on the desk.

"Here is your food," he says. Then he looks around carefully, placing his finger to his lips for you to be quiet. He takes out a small slip of paper and a pencil. He prints: GO BEFORE IT'S TOO LATE—TONIGHT. He points to your watch and holds up three fingers. You guess that he means 3 a.m.

The monk then crumples up the piece of paper, pops it into his mouth, and swallows it. Then he slips back out the door and is gone.

Turn to page 33.

42

You pull the dark, heavy curtains on the hotel windows shut. Then you lie down on the bed and stretch out. You are asleep almost immediately.

You're not sure how long you've been asleep when something wakes you up. You sit up and listen. The door to the bathroom is slightly open, making a narrow rectangle of bright light on the other side of the darkened room. You can hear water running.

You start toward the bathroom. As you enter, someone jumps out from behind you and pulls a bag over your head. You try to call out, but you can't. Then you hear another person and some muttered conversation in what sounds like Japanese. *Japanese?*

Whoever they are, they tie your hands and feet, lift you up, and lower you into what must be a laundry basket. Sheets and towels are then piled on top of you. You're unable to move.

As far as you can tell, they are rolling you out of your room and down the hall, in the opposite direction from the main elevator bank, most likely to a service elevator.

With the bag over your head and the sheets piled on top of you, you can hardly breathe. You just hope that you don't suffocate before you get to where they are taking you.

Before long you lose consciousness.

Turn to page 49.

McFee drives with one hand and pulls a military hat out from under the seat. It has two stars on it.

"I only wear this on ceremonial occasions," he says. "Out at the camp we're very informal. Nobody worries about rank. It's not like being in the army or anything."

Twenty minutes later, you are rolling through a heavily wooded area.

"It's not far now," General McFee says. "Oh, and before we get there, you have to decide whether you want night training or day training."

"What's the difference?" you ask.

"Well, for one thing, with night training you're not going to see daylight for a couple of weeks. We train you to live in the dark, operate in the dark, and fight in the dark. Day training is somewhat more conventional."

"I have to decide right away?" you ask.

"Yes. I know I'm not giving you much time," he says, as the jeep turns onto an unmarked road that winds through a thick woods.

You come out at the edge of a field around which are several barnlike structures and a building that is clearly a barracks.

"Have you decided?" General McFee asks.

Night training certainly sounds like fun, you speculate. At the very least, it would be exciting. On the other hand, it might be less riskier to pick day training. You don't want to get involved in something you'll regret.

If you pick night training, turn to page 111.

If you pick day training, turn to page 108.

Kyo leads you up to the only visible door to the cube-shaped building and pushes you inside, closing the door behind you.

The inside looks like an oversized war room of some major power. Large data screens run along the walls, and dozens of technicians sit in front of computer terminals. An unusually tall, heavyset Oriental dressed in an overly elaborate military officer's uniform sits on a kind of throne atop a raised platform in the center. Somehow you don't have to be told that he's Kong-yi.

Kong-yi lifts his bulk and descends the wide stairway on the side of the platform. At the same time, you realize that two guards armed with American M16 rifles have moved in behind you.

"Ah, there you are!" Kong-yi exclaims in a deep, booming voice. "I've heard great things about your abilities. You will be my first *super warrior* . . . once you are properly programed."

"Programed! I don't *want* to be programed."

"But you must! It is important to my plans— plans that will soon bring about the unification of North and South Korea. Then I will rule all of Korea! But first, I need your help."

One of the guards suddenly hits you on the head from behind. You aren't completely knocked out, but you're too stunned to fight back. You should have escaped earlier, when you had the chance.

The End

They push you up a short flight of stairs and then down a long stone passageway. You come out on an embankment along the river. It is night. The lights along the opposite shore reflect in the water, and off to the left in the distance, a steady stream of headlights is crossing a bridge.

"This is the end of the line for you!" the man says, as Moto raises his gun to your head.

Suddenly there is a blur from above, and a dark figure knocks the gun away just as he fires. The sound deafens you for a moment. Several other black-clad figures drop from above and land on the embankment. The man who questioned you dives into the river as Moto tries to fire at the dark figures.

You move as fast as you can, catching Moto's wrist with an openhanded kung fu chop. The blow sends his gun flying into the air and out over the river. A few seconds later, you hear the splash as it hits the water. Moto and Matsuki run away down the embankment. You let them go. One of the dark-suited figures comes over to you.

"You are very good!" the man says. Then he starts to move back into the darkness.

"Where is Ling?" you call out after him.

There is silence for a few moments. Then the figure returns.

"Who are you? Why you ask such question?" he says in a heavy accent.

"I'm a friend of hers," you say. "I have to find out if she's all right."

"Come," he says.

Go on to the next page.

You follow him down along the river. Three more fighters fall in beside you. They lead you to a small pier where a large cabin cruiser is tied up, its engine throbbing and sounding very efficient. They take you below and down to the main cabin. There they take off their night camouflage hoods. There is something about them that reminds you of Ling's fighters in China.

"You American, right? I think you the one Ling speak about. She say you have much talent."

"Where is she?" you ask.

"She's up in Sorak Mountains. There are bad men there. Have false monastery, have evil plans. Ling mean to defeat them."

"Can I see her?" you ask.

"She no come back here. Go to Macao after mission. We help you here as much as we can."

You remember the instructions that agents McKenna and Borkin sent you—you are to activate the transmitter in your wristwatch if you locate Ling. You have enough information now, you think. At least you know that she's alive. But something tells you to wait. If you could only talk to Ling herself and find out what this is all about.

*If you activate your watch signal,
turn to page 92.*

If you decide to wait, turn to page 52.

When you come to, you realize you are in a basement somewhere. The bag is off your head, and you are tied to a chair. A man is slapping you gently on the face to bring you around.

When your eyes can focus, you see that the man in front of you is not Oriental.

"Don't lie to us," he says. "We know that you were sent here by the CIA to spy on our operation."

"I'm just a student," you protest. "I'm here to study tae kwon do."

"Nonsense! Just a student? Is that why you are staying in one of the most expensive hotels in Seoul? Unless you tell us everything, we will hold you prisoner in a small cell where you will starve until you talk," he hisses, as two Japanese men enter the basement room. "Moto and Matsuki here will see to that!"

Turn to page 110.

The next morning you wake with a start and look at the clock. You've slept too late to catch Chung's bus for the mountains. You are glad about that—before you went to sleep last night you formed another plan in your mind. The first thing you need to do is find a bank that will change your Korean won into American dollars.

Yun was right—you get about thirty thousand dollars, all of which you change again into international traveler's checks.

Later, as you come around the side of the hill behind the hotel, you spot Borkin from the CIA and Chung from the tae kwon do school hiding behind some bushes, watching the front of the hotel. Borkin and Chung together? Whatever they're up to, you want no part of it. You quickly duck down and back off before they see you, then run back to the main boulevard and take a cab to the train station.

Leaving all your things at the hotel, you take a train to Kunsan, a port city 110 miles to the south. You go down to the harbor where you have no trouble finding a passenger ship leaving for Hong Kong. Using your winnings, you take the most luxurious cabin they have and settle down to enjoy the voyage.

You hope your friends from your last trip to Hong Kong are still there. They were also friends of Ling. Maybe *they* know what's going on. You remind yourself to send Billy Baxter and your mom a postcard when you get there.

The End

"Where is she?" Borkin asks.

"Ling? Don't worry, she's alive somewhere in this part of Korea," you say.

"Exactly *where* in this part of Korea?"

"Well, I don't know *exactly!*" you protest.

Borkin takes off his hat and throws it down on the pier.

"Sorry," you say. "But I thought—"

"You mean you activated the entire SATNET system and you don't know *exactly* where she is?"

"But I thought you wanted to know if she's alive and—"

"Never mind that. You shouldn't have activated the signal unless you actually *saw* her. You received your instructions. You should know what you're supposed to do."

"I . . . I didn't realize. I'll try again," you say.

"Forget it. You're off the case!" Borkin shouts. "Use your return ticket and go home."

With that, he stomps back down the pier and gets into the helicopter. You watch as it climbs into the sky and disappears.

You feel bad that you disappointed Borkin, but you're glad that Ling is alive. Maybe one day you'll get to see her again.

You find your way back to the hotel. In the morning, you check out and take a cab to the airport. Somehow this was not the trip you expected it to be.

The End

You decide to wait before activating the signal. You rest for a while. They serve you a thin soup with small cubes of bean cake, a kind of light cheese made from soybeans instead of milk. The man in charge introduces himself as Wu Bai, Ling's chief assistant.

About an hour later, one of the men comes down from above, talking excitedly in Chinese.

"This is our radio operator," Wu Bai says. "He just received a coded message from Ling. He sent a message back that you are here."

"Then I can see her?"

"That is being arranged," Wu Bai says. "Before that, we go upriver."

Soon you feel the vibration as the motor goes into high gear and the cabin cruiser begins to move.

You go up on deck with Wu Bai. It is early dawn, and the lights of the city still sparkle against a backdrop of crimson spreading in the east.

Turn to page 68.

You leave your bags on the bed and carefully lock the door to your room. Then you take the elevator back down to the lobby and go outside, ready to explore.

The sides of the four story buildings are thick with vertical signs—all in strange Korean lettering. You look in the shop windows. They are well stocked with radios, VCRs, women's shoes, handbags, and jewelry, and men's suits and custommade shirts.

You come to a shop that has a large photo filling its front window. The photo shows two figures in white tae kwon do uniforms. One of the figures is airborne, throwing a snap-kick at the other.

You go inside expecting to find a school. Instead you discover the place is a large bookstore specializing in the martial arts. You browse around. Most of the books are in Korean, but you finally find one in English. A man standing next to you watches you thumb through it.

Turn to page 64.

54

You follow Pak out of the bookstore and down the crowded street to the corner. He turns left onto a side street that is almost deserted.

"Don't get worried," he says. "This is just a shortcut. We'll be back on the main street in a block or two."

In fact, you can see a busy intersection not far up ahead.

Suddenly two black-garbed figures appear in front of the two of you—and another two from behind. They have you surrounded. Pak pushes you back against a wall at the side of the street.

"Stay here," he says. "This won't take long."

Two of the dark figures rush at him. Pak is a blur in the air for a moment, and the figures fall to the ground, groaning and holding their heads.

The other two are more cautious. They approach him warily, one of them trying to get behind him. Pak seems to strike forward and backward at the same time. One of the attackers bounces off the wall on the other side of the street and sinks to the ground. The other, holding his leg, limps toward the intersection up ahead.

"Wow! That was great!" you exclaim.

"There will be others coming—more skilled, I'm afraid. The one limping was trying to lead us into an ambush."

"But the main street was just up ahead."

"It would seem so," he says. "But a block can be a long way to go with gunmen shooting from the windows."

"Gunmen?"

Turn to page 106.

56

Later in the afternoon, but just how much later you can't tell, you come to. Your head is throbbing.

You struggle to your feet, gingerly feeling the cut on the side of your head. All is quiet. The figures in black are all gone. So are Chung and most of the tae kwon do students. There are three of them left, sitting and nursing their wounds by the side of the road. The bus is a skeleton of blackened, twisted wreckage.

You go over to the remaining students. They are arguing in Korean. You can't understand what they are saying, but from their hand motions you guess that they are trying to decide whether to go forward or back down the road.

One of them gets up and starts limping back the way you came, gesturing for you to follow him. The other two start off in the opposite direction. You don't want to be left there alone. You'll have to decide quickly which way to go.

If you follow the limping student down the road, turn to page 94.

If you go forward with the other two students, turn to page 35.

"I'd rather go directly to Korea," you tell the agents.

"Okay," McKenna says. "In a week or so, a small package will be dropped off here. It will contain everything you'll need."

The two men leave. Your mother watches them through the front window as they cross the lawn and get into their car.

The next day at school you find your friend Billy Baxter and tell him about the two men.

"They came to see me, too," Billy says. "But I'm through with the martial arts. I still have nightmares about what happened to us in China. My interest now is computers—and only computers! If I were you, I wouldn't have anything to do with those men."

"But Ling may be in trouble," you say. "If it hadn't been for her, we'd never have gotten home."

"All right, go then—but be careful! And send me a postcard."

A week later, a package is waiting for you when you get home from school. It contains plane tickets—round-trip—to the Korean capital, Seoul, a list of Korean expressions, the signal wristwatch, and a packet of Korean money.

When the school term ends and your summer vacation begins, you pack up your bags and take a bus to the airport. Soon you are on a long, direct flight to Seoul.

Turn to page 6.

"Kong-yi's main stronghold is not far from here, and he has his own personal air force, as well as some advanced weapons developed for him by Chong Kyu Pyun, director of the Pyun Corporation," Ling says.

She suddenly stops talking and jumps to her feet, motioning for you to be quiet. There is a buzzing sound in the distance. It's in the sky to the northwest and to the left of the hill. Through the trees you catch a momentary glimpse of three saucer-shaped airships heading in your direction.

"What are those?" you ask.

"Kong-yi's helicopters. They'll be searching for us with infrared scanners."

"Those are helicopters? They look more like flying saucers."

"They are a radically new design," Ling says. "They're from the Pyun Corporation. Hurry! We are almost to the top of the hill. We have to get to the other side."

You follow Ling as she dashes up the trail. When you are almost to the top, there is a tremendous explosion from somewhere behind, sending a ball of flame up into the sky.

"Quick, in here!" she shouts.

Turn to page 16.

"I think I'll hide here in the village," you say.

"Okay, then. Good luck," Ling says, gathering up her papers. In a matter of seconds she is out the back door and gone.

One of the Koreans shows you where to crawl under the floorboards. "Space for heating in winter," he says. "Now good place to hide."

A short time later you hear the tread of boots on the thin floor directly above your head. From the sounds you guess that Kong-yi's men are running to the back door after Ling. Then you hear gunshots from that direction. You hope Ling got away.

You try to crawl deeper in the narrow space. In the process, you scrape your watch on the bare ground underneath you. You look at the watch and realize that the time-setting knob has been pulled all the way out.

Sometime later your Korean friend comes back and helps you crawl out from under the floorboards.

"Bad men gone," he says.

You go outside and walk back to the river. The boat that belonged to the Chinese is no longer there. You wonder what happened to Wu Bai and the crew.

Then you notice everyone is pointing up. The sky is filled with parachutes drifting down toward the village.

You are about to run and hide again, but the man who hid you before shakes his head. "Those regular Korean army troops," he says. "Recognize uniform. They come to help."

Turn to page 4.

You climb into the hole, using the rope to ease your way down. You haven't gone far when you come out on a ledge high above a huge cavern. It looks like it's at least a hundred feet to the bottom. It is dimly lit, but you can make out rows of saucer-shaped machines lined along the floor of the cavern.

Ling is slowly lowering her pack to the bottom on the end of a second rope.

"Someone is coming up above," you say.

"All right, let's get out of here," she says. "We have just enough time to get off this mountain before it blows."

You go first, scrambling back up the shaft, using the rope to pull yourself up. Halfway to the top, the rope suddenly comes loose, and you fall backward, crashing into Ling. The two of you land in a heap back on the ledge.

When you try to stand up again, you find that you can hardly move. You must have broken your leg in the fall.

Ling does her best to get you up the shaft to safety. But when you are halfway up, the mountain explodes, along with you, Ling, Kong-yi, and his building!

The End

Fifteen hours later the plane lands at Kimpo International Airport, a number of miles from the city of Seoul. You get off the plane and walk into the morning sunshine with Joan. The airport is a large one, with modern, glass-walled administration buildings. The airport itself is surrounded by rolling farmland.

"My father should be here to meet me," Joan says. "We'll be glad to give you a ride to the city."

The customs people all seem to know your new friend, and at her side you breeze through all the formalities. A long limousine is waiting at the curb outside the customs building. A uniformed chauffeur gets out and snaps his hand to the brim of his cap in an almost military salute when Joan arrives. She talks with him in Korean. You can't tell what they are saying, but you can tell that she is upset.

"My father has been called away on business," she says, turning to you. "I'm sorry. I wish you could have met him."

The chauffeur puts your bags into the trunk along with Joan's and then opens the rear door. The two of you climb into the backseat.

The limousine speeds away from the airport, turning onto a broad highway leading to the capital.

Go on to the next page.

"Where are you staying?" Joan asks.

"I don't know," you say. "Do you know a good hotel, something not too expensive?"

"I'd recommend the Seoul Hilton," she says. "It's near all the major sights. I have friends there, and I can get you a special rate."

As the limo gets close to the city, it slows down and begins to inch along in traffic.

"You see," Joan says, laughing. "We are up-to-date in everything, even traffic jams."

She reaches over and presses a button on the inside of the door next to you. The window rolls down. You stick your head out and see a skyline of tall skyscrapers gleaming in the sun inside a ring of green mountains up ahead.

Soon the traffic speeds up a bit, and you go across a bridge spanning a wide river into the main part of the city. The city looks modern, as modern as any in America. But there are also some very ancient-looking buildings—structures from some distant past that specialized in large, curved, tile-covered roofs. Joan points out the *Namdae-Mun,* or Great South Gate, a remnant of the high wall that once surrounded the entire city.

Then she speaks to the driver on the intercom. You can make out the word *Hilton* in the conversation. The limo turns to the right and goes toward one of the mountains up ahead—a mountain topped by a modern television tower. Then you pull up to the entrance of a tall skyscraper sheathed with smoked glass.

Turn to page 8.

"You are American?" he asks in accented English.

"Uh, yes I am," you answer.

"My name is Pak Sik," he says, grabbing your hand and shaking it with a strong grip. "Are you studying the martial arts?"

"Yes . . . that is, I haven't started my studies here yet."

"Perhaps I could recommend a good *kwan*," Pak says.

"Kwan?"

"A school for tae kwon do," he answers. "I could take you over to one and introduce you. I know the instructor well. It's not far away."

"I just arrived by plane from the United States, and—"

"It won't take long," Pak interjects. "There's an exhibition of tae kwon do techniques going on there now."

You think about Pak's offer for a moment. You realize that jet lag is catching up with you—you feel a little dizzy and wobbly in the knees. Rest is important, but you might miss an important opportunity.

If you decide to go with Pak Sik,
turn to page 54.

If you decide to go back to the hotel to rest,
turn to page 12.

66

About an hour later, there is a loud knock at your door. Agents Borkin and McKenna are there. They push their way into your room.

"What is this about leaving before you've completed your mission?" Borkin demands.

"I've heard that Ling is now an assassin for a terrorist group called the Red Dragon Society," you say. "And if—"

"Nonsense!" McKenna interrupts. "It may be true that she's infiltrated some organization—but only as an undercover agent for us. We still need to know where she is."

"I guess the problem is that you don't have enough training for this mission," Borkin says to you. "You really should have taken our special training program in Maryland. I think it would be best if we fly you back there on a military transport."

"We have a car waiting," McKenna adds.

They gather up your belongings and escort you out to the front of the hotel. There you climb into the back of a military-green car and are taken to an air force base 15 miles out of the city. Before you know it, you are on a plane flying back to the United States.

You land at an air force base outside Washington, DC. A jeep is waiting there for you as you step off the plane. When you get in, it immediately heads for the CIA training camp in Springview, Maryland.

"My name is General McFee," the driver says.

Turn to page 43.

"I have to stay here until I find Ling," you say.

"I can't make you change your mind?" Pak asks.

"No, I'm afraid not. I gave my word."

"That's too bad," Pak says, pulling out a revolver and pointing it at you.

He opens a trapdoor in the center of the floor. You can hear rushing water far below as he shoves you toward the opening.

"If you can hold your breath for a mile or so underwater, you might make it to the river," he says, pushing you in.

You try holding your breath—but not for very long! This mission is your last.

The End

You travel for several hours to the northeast as the river winds through a beautiful landscape of rolling hills. You spot several waterfalls on overhanging bluffs. Then, up ahead, you see a small village spread out along the bank. The boat stops there, and you follow Wu Bai as he jumps into the shallow water and wades ashore. You come up on dry land between two fishing boats resting on a narrow stretch of gravel beach. Then you start down a dirt road with clusters of one-story houses on both sides. The houses are made of hard-baked clay and have roofs of straw. Beyond the village, you see rice fields stretching to the base of a tall hill covered with cedar and pine.

The women here in the village are wearing colorful, high-waisted dresses of which you saw only a few while you were in Seoul. Some of them are carrying large bundles of wash on their heads. Others have babies strapped to their backs with wide sashes. A farmer, dressed in plain work clothes—a white shirt and pants with a blue vest—trudges past you. He is carrying a large wooden frame on his shoulders piled high with dry branches.

You follow Wu Bai to the front of one of the houses.

"Take off your shoes and leave them by the door," he says as he slides back a panel to let you in.

Turn to page 30.

"How much is this in American money?" you ask Yun.

He thinks for a minute, rubbing his chin. "Maybe thirty thousand dollars," he says, shrugging his shoulders.

You leave the casino in a daze and take a cab back to the hotel.

Back in your suite, as you get ready to go to bed, the phone starts to ring. You pick it up, but there is no one there. You hang it up. It rings again almost at once.

"Hello?" you say.

"This Kenzo Ohki," a voice says. "Sorry not at casino when you come. Some trouble. Thank you for returning book. Still need information on Ling woman. Will call again soon when out of hospital."

Kenzo hangs up. Before you can climb into bed, the phone rings again. This time it's Chung reminding you about the bus leaving in the morning.

The next call is from Borkin of the CIA. You have no idea where he is calling from.

"The situation is urgent," he says. "I need information about Ling as soon as possible."

"I've only been here a few hours!" you protest. "And how did you find out which hotel I'm in?"

"I had my office check all the hotels in Seoul," he says.

You are about to tell him about the money you won, but decide not to.

After Borkin's call, you take the phone off the hook and go to sleep.

Turn to page 50.

Medics are bringing a slim Japanese man out on a stretcher from the same door. He seems to be alive, though you notice some blood. He looks down the street and spots you. He must be the one who left you the note at the hotel. The man tries to push himself up on the stretcher and say something to you, but he collapses back down. A small crumpled piece of paper drops from his hand and falls to the sidewalk as they load him into the ambulance. The two policemen get back into their squad car and zoom off, followed by the ambulance.

Everything is quiet again. No one else has come out of the White Crane. The paper the man dropped skips along in the wind as you run after it. You uncrumple the paper and gasp in surprise. It's the picture of Ling, the one that was taken from your bag at the hotel! You turn it over and see that several words in Korean have been scribbled on the back.

You look inside the doorway of the White Crane and see a long, dimly lit stairway leading down. If this is a restaurant, it doesn't look too appetizing.

You wonder—the man they took away in the ambulance may have friends inside who can tell you about Ling. On the other hand, you could be walking into a dangerous situation. Maybe you should turn around and go back to the hotel where you can think things out.

If you go down the stairway, turn to page 86.

If you go back to the hotel, turn to page 23.

You sleep fitfully and wake up sometime after dark. You get out of bed and, still groggy, walk over to the window. Outside the sparkling lights of the city with its many skyscrapers spread out before you in a vast panorama.

You look at your watch. It says 6:15 a.m. That must be the time back in the States right now. You look around and find a clock in the suite. It says 8:15 *p.m.* Your body is still working on your old time schedule. You reset your watch to the new time and get dressed.

Suddenly you feel very alone in this distant land. At least you have a return ticket in your pocket. You reach in to make sure it's still there. It is, and so is the card that Pak Sik gave you. It has the address of the Yum Duk Kwan. You feel rested and up to more exploring now.

You go down the elevator and through the lobby. As you do, one of the hotel clerks comes running over to you.

"Message left for you," he says, handing you a slip of paper.

The handwriting is crude, as though the writer had just recently learned English—and not too well. The spelling isn't too good either, but you can make it out. It says:

"Have information on Ling. Come to White Crane restaurant on Taep Street."

Go on to the next page.

Who knows you are at the hotel? you wonder. Joan Pyun, of course, but *her* English was perfect, at least in conversation. And you didn't tell Pak at the bookstore where you were staying—unless he followed you.

The front of the hotel is bustling with activity. Crowds of well-dressed people, a few of them obviously American, are getting in and out of fancy cars and limousines. You spot a line of cabs a short way down the street. You walk down and get into the backseat of one of them.

"Odiekaseyo?" the driver says.

"Do you speak English?" you ask.

"Oh, yes, I speak English well," he answers. "I worked many years with the American army. I was asking where you wanted to go."

You really want to go to the kwan that Pak recommended before you do anything else, but the writer of the note just might have some important information about Ling.

If you go to the kwan, turn to page 14.

If you go to the address on the note,
turn to page 91.

"I think I'd like to go to Japan," you tell McFee.

"All right, we'll have a seat for you on a flight leaving tonight," he says.

At ten a.m. local time the next day, you land at Haneda International Airport near Tokyo. You go through customs, then look for a taxicab to take you to the city. Several tough-looking Japanese men surround you at the cab stand.

"We know you come here to look for Chinese woman named Ling," one of them says in heavily accented English.

"How do you know that?" you ask.

"We get tip yesterday that you arrive today looking for this woman," he says.

This makes you wonder what's really going on. You start to duck away, but he grabs your arm.

"The situation here very confusing. We need you to talk with boss of Tokyo Yakuza," he says.

A Toyota minivan pulls up at the curb next to you, and the side door slides open. There are two more Yakuza men inside, as well as the driver, and they all have what look to be guns under their leather jackets. You have no choice but to get in.

The van heads toward Tokyo but soon turns off onto a winding side road. After another 20 minutes, it goes through an elaborate gate and into a parklike estate. Up ahead, on a high hill is a medieval-looking building painted white with a sloping tile roof.

"That old castle now headquarters of Yakuza," one of the men says.

Turn to page 113.

You stay where you are and watch as Kenzo disappears into the kitchen. Two of the men go after him, while the third one heads for your table. You can tell from the expression on his face that he means business.

Just as he gets to you, you grab one of the drinks from the table and throw it in his face. Then you run for the door.

You glance back and see that the people in the restaurant are slowing him down—sticking out their feet and trying to trip him.

You get through the green curtain and bound up the stairs three steps at a time. You run outside and down the street.

At the corner you see the cab that brought you here—its motor is running and the back door is open. You dive in, and the driver roars off before you even close the door.

Soon you are on one of the main streets.

"I had to come back," the driver says. "I knew you'd probably need a fast getaway from that place. Back to the hotel?"

"No!" you say. "Take me straight to the airport. I have my return ticket with me. I'll send the money to the hotel and have them send me my bags."

You're glad to have escaped from the restaurant with your life. You might not be so lucky the next time. You thank the driver and spend the rest of the night in the airport, waiting for the next available flight back to the United States.

The End

You remember your kung fu training. You jump forward, aiming an openhanded blow at the side of Chung's neck. With one swift motion he moves sideways and grabs your arm, pulling it forward in the direction it was going in a wide, curving motion. You lose your balance and tumble to the ground.

"That is an example of a soft technique," he says. "Tae kwon do uses both hard and soft methods."

Go on to the next page.

For many weeks, Chung demonstrates for you each kick and each technique. You practice until you have them all down. In addition, you fall into the regular routine of the monastery. However, there *are* things that worry you, like the sounds late at night of low-flying planes or helicopters. And the noises that you sometimes hear in the direction of the strange, cube-shaped building.

One day Kyo stops you and Chung on your way to practice.

"Kong-yi is ready to see your student," Kyo says to Chung.

"Already?" he says. "I thought—"

"Never mind," Kyo snaps. "Kong-yi must not be kept waiting."

"As you say," Chung says.

Chung remains behind as Kyo leads you up the winding trail to the cube-shaped building on the hillside above the monastery.

You suddenly get a premonition that something terrible is going to happen to you there. You can't imagine what, but from the expression on Chung's face, this may be your *last* chance to make a break for it and get away.

With your tae kwon do training, you are sure that Kyo couldn't stop you. But if you run away, will you be able to find your way over the mountains to safety?

If you keep going to meet Kong-yi in the cube-shaped building, turn to page 44.

If you make a break for it, turn to page 101.

It's so quiet that soon you begin to hear the blood rushing through the veins in your head. It sounds like a waterfall heard from a distance.

You sit there trying to stay alert, but it's not easy. You begin to feel very alone. You wish you'd never gotten yourself involved in this whole thing.

Finally you hear the door open and footsteps coming into the room.

"I'm Sergeant Dawson," a voice says in the darkness. "In the next two weeks you will become a nocturnal animal, able to see in the dimmest light, able to hear the faintest sound."

He is right. For two weeks you live in total darkness and go on night maneuvers in the woods with others in the same program. You all wear black costumes like Ninja and learn to move soundlessly and invisibly through the night.

After two weeks, you finish your training.

"You have been assigned to track down a Chinese woman named Ling," General McFee says. "You have the advantage of knowing her personally. Right now, we have possible sightings in Singapore and Macao. Where would you like to look?"

Without any more information, either choice seems as good as the other. You don't, however, have the luxury of time. You have to make a decision right now.

*If you decide to go to Singapore,
turn to page 115.*

If you decide to go to Macao, turn to page 118.

"I just thought I'd—" you start.

"I know," the man says. "My name is Shin Chung. My friend, Pak Sik, described you. I've been expecting you. You are an American, right?"

"Yes," you say. "I just got to Korea this morning."

"I suspect that you know something of the martial arts already," Chung says.

"I've studied kung fu in China," you say.

"Kung fu very good—goes back to Shaolin Temple in ancient China. Our tradition even older, goes back two thousand years. Also, we learn much from the Chinese and Japanese methods. We call our art tae kwon do, but in this kwan it is a mixture of karate, kung fu, and our own Korean styles."

"That sounds good," you say.

"If you would like to study with us, we can enroll you."

"When do I start?" you say.

"Part of our kwan is here at this location. Our main center is in the Sorak Mountains, where the students live and practice tae kwon do full-time. Here in the city, we have daily classes for all levels, and the students live at home. The choice is yours."

You remember that you are here to search for Ling. She could be anywhere—just as easily in the mountains as in Seoul. The choice really *is* yours.

If you decide to stay in the city,
turn to page 112.

If you decide to study in the Sorak Mountains,
turn to page 21.

"I'm not ready to leave yet," you whisper to the monk.

You hear rustling in the dark, and then silence. The monk must have left. You hope that you made the right decision. You try to go back to sleep, but you just toss and turn for a couple of hours.

Finally, sometime before dawn, Kyo appears at the door and turns on a light.

"It is almost time for early meditation," he says. "The monk's robe in the dresser will be appropriate. I will return in ten minutes and escort you to the meditation hall."

You stumble out of bed and take a quick, cold shower. You look in the dresser and find the monk's robe. There are also a number of white tae kwon do uniforms.

When Kyo returns, you follow him in the predawn darkness to the hall of the Buddha, now dimly lit by candles in front of the statue of the Buddha itself. Kyo shows you where to sit, crosslegged, in the front row.

The others start a low, rhythmic chant. You join in with them. After a while, you begin to feel lightheaded, but not drowsy. Your body seems to be filling with a strange energy. At the same time, the statue in front of you appears to grow in size and shimmer brighter and brighter until it seems sheathed in flame.

The sound of a gong snaps you back to reality. The other students get up and file out of the hall. You don't see Kyo, but you guess that you are supposed to follow the others.

Turn to page 37.

You follow the man in the tuxedo to the side of the hall and up a circular metal stairway that leads to an office with a broad window overlooking the floor of the casino. You realize that it must have one-way glass, since you saw it as a large mirror from down below.

An Oriental woman is standing there looking down intently at the gamblers. She is dressed in a strapless evening gown made of a shimmering, silver-colored material. Her shiny black hair is parted in the middle and pulled back into a long ponytail.

The man in the tuxedo who brought you upstairs whispers something in her ear.

"Please be seated. I'll be with you in a moment," she says to you in perfect English. She only looks away from the window for a second. She says something to the man, pointing down at the floor below. He leaves hurriedly, and then the woman turns to look at you.

"You asked about Kenzo," she says. "Poor Kenzo, one of our most faithful workers. He's in the hospital recovering from the effects of a street brawl of some sort."

"It was in a restaurant, actually. He dropped this," you say, handing her the small notebook. "I thought it might be valuable."

"Kenzo will be most grateful," she says, thumbing quickly through it. "You deserve a reward."

"I don't really want one," you say. "I'm just glad to—"

"No," she interrupts, "I insist."

Turn to page 96.

"I'm afraid I can't accept your offer," you say.

"I understand," Pyun says.

He calls in the driver and tells him to take you back to the city, adding something in Korean.

"Thanks for the offer anyway," you say, and follow the driver out of the building.

You get in the limousine, and slowly it starts toward the gate. Immediately you start feeling dizzy. But before you lose consciousness, you realize that the back of the car must be filling up with an odorless and probably deadly gas.

Before it reaches the guardhouse, the limo makes a left turn into the field on the side of the driveway. It stops next to a deep trench where the driver has been instructed to dump your lifeless body.

The End

Despite Joan's warning, you start your classes at the Yum Duk Kwan. Each day you jog the dozen or so blocks back and forth from the school to the hotel. Every time you try to find out how much your hotel bill will cost, they just say, "It's been taken care of."

But by whom? you wonder.

On your way to school, after you've been studying the many techniques of tae kwon do for a little over a month, Joan's limousine pulls up at the curb alongside you.

"Miss Pyun needs see you," the driver says, getting out and holding open the door. There's something not quite right about the way he says it, but you go anyway. The limo then drives out of the city.

"She at the factory of her father," the driver announces through the intercom.

After a half-hour drive, you go through a gate in a high chain link fence. It takes another ten minutes of driving to get to one of the enormous five-story factory buildings in the distance.

The driver opens the car door for you, then leads you into the building and down a long narrow hallway to an office.

"Mr. Pyun will see you right away," the secretary in the outer office says.

"But I came here to see Joan."

The secretary gets up and opens a large double door, motioning for you to enter.

Turn to page 22.

"That is a flying side kick," Chung says. "It's the trademark of tae kwon do. You will learn this as well as the front kick and the back kick. These we call direct kicks. There are other kicks with the body turning in the air. We call those circular kicks. Some of these are the wheel kick, the crescent kick, and especially the roundhouse kick."

You stand there, trying to keep it all straight.

"Ah, you look confused," he says, patting you on the shoulder. "They will all become clear to you as you practice."

"It does seem complicated right now," you say.

Chung smiles and goes on. "But before you learn these kicks, you must understand the difference between the *soft* arts and the *hard* arts. In the hard arts, the enemy is attacked directly with whatever force is available—guns, knives, anything. If the fighter finds himself completely unarmed, he or she can use punches, openhanded strikes, blows from the knees, elbows, and above all, kicks. On the other hand, the principle of the soft arts is never to oppose an attacking force. Instead, use the oncoming force itself to defeat the attacker. Here, I will show you. Try to make a direct strike against me."

Turn to page 76.

You go down the stairway of the White Crane, then through a green curtain at the bottom. The inside of the restaurant, a large, dimly lit room with a vaulted ceiling, is a shambles. Tables and chairs are overturned, and the floor is littered with broken glass. Two Koreans, probably waiters, are standing in front of a long bar at one side looking dazed. The place is otherwise empty of people.

"Big fight here," one of the waiters says. "One Japanese man and many Chinese. Japanese man outnumbered but make good fight. Take him away in ambulance."

"I saw the ambulance leave," you say.

"Chinese leave through back door in kitchen. Other people also—they go before police arrive. Not want trouble. Japanese man come in, sit over there," he says, pointing to the far corner.

You go over and look under the overturned table. Wedged underneath is a small green notebook. You pull it out and open the cover. The first page has something written in Japanese. You ask the other waiter, an older man, if he can make it out.

"Japanese make us learn their language when they occupy our country many years ago," he says, taking the notebook. "It is a name and address. I would read this as 'Kenzo Ohki, 2084 Wangsan Street, Seoul.' Rest of the notebook also in Japanese, but some kind of code. Think this type of code used by Yakuza, Japanese gangsters."

Go on to the next page.

How and why did the Japanese man get your photo of Ling? you wonder. And why did the Chinese attack him?

The green notebook certainly provides you with a good lead. Perhaps you should go to the address inside. However, you are feeling tired—your body hasn't had the chance to adjust to the 14-hour time difference between Korea and the United States. Perhaps you should go back to your hotel room and take a nap.

If you go to the address in the notebook, turn to page 26.

If you go back to your hotel, turn to page 42.

"Right now I'd rather go back to Seoul," you say.

"There is a dirt road from this village that leads to the main highway. Woo Hi Lee will show you the way," Chung says.

A girl about ten years old enters the room. Chung talks with her in Korean.

"Hi Lee doesn't speak any English, but I've told her what to do," he says. "Before you leave, she will get you something to eat."

Hi Lee bows to you and smiles. You say good-bye to Chung and follow her into the other room where she serves you rice, fish, and bean cake. She also gives you some hot tea. You don't realize how hungry you are until you start eating.

After your meal, Hi Lee leads you out of the village along a road that goes southwest, straight across the valley. You walk for over an hour. Hi Lee skips alongside carrying a basket and collecting wildflowers as the two of you walk.

Eventually you come to a modern highway. You wait there for a while until you see a large truck coming from the east. Hi Lee holds up her flowers and waves with her other hand. The truck comes to a stop several yards down the highway. You and Hi Lee run over to it. She talks to the driver in Korean and hands him the flowers. The driver laughs and motions for you to get in.

"*Komap Simnida*. Thank you," you say to Hi Lee. You remember it from the list of expressions that Borkin gave you before you left. Hi Lee waves good-bye as the truck starts off down the highway.

Turn to page 104.

"Do you know where she is?" you ask.

"She was recently in the Yokohama Chinatown, but we believe that she has now gone to Korea. We expect her to come back to Japan sooner or later."

"I can't do much, then, I'm afraid, until I see her," you say.

"Ah, but you can. I've arranged for you to study the techniques of the ancient Ninja with all the best teachers. After that, and after you talk with Ling, we have a choice position for you in our overseas operations."

"And suppose I don't want to help you?" you say.

"This castle is famous for many things. One of them is the dungeon deep below," he says. "If we must, we will keep you there until you decide otherwise."

If he puts it that way, you reason, then what choice do you really have? For the first time, you look upon your interest in the martial arts with regret.

The End

"I'm going to the White Crane restaurant on Taep Street," you say to the cabdriver.

"The White Crane?" he repeats. "You don't really want to go there. Not safe!"

"I'm afraid I have to. I'm trying to locate a friend, and someone there may have some information."

"I'll take you there if you want me to, but I can't wait around for you near that place."

The driver goes down a crowded main street for several blocks and then turns into a poorer neighborhood. The streets become narrow and almost deserted. Finally the driver stops in front of a doorway set into a plain cement wall. There is a small picture of a white crane over the door, but without any lettering, Korean or otherwise.

"This is it," the driver says.

"I don't suppose you would go in with me. I'll pay you," you say.

"Not on a bet," he says.

You give the driver his fare, and he goes speeding away.

There is a long dark stairway leading down when you look inside the doorway. You can hear voices and raucous laughter coming from below. You go down slowly, wondering why you are doing this.

Turn to page 11.

You decide to activate the transmitter in your watch. You pull the time-setting knob free from the watch. You can't hear anything, but you know that it's communicating the proper signal. Or is it? you wonder. The thought crosses your mind that this whole thing could be some kind of hoax. Regardless, you'll just have to wait and see what happens.

A few minutes later, one of the fighters comes running below deck, hollering something in Chinese. All of them look at you.

"You have device—send out signal? It make interference on ship's instruments," he says.

You're not sure what to tell them. "Well, I—" you start.

From the expression on your face, they can tell that you're guilty.

"We must go. Leave you here!" one of them says.

They quickly but politely escort you to the deck. As soon as you are ashore, the engine goes into full power and the boat roars away from the pier.

You stand there for a while wondering what to do. Then there is the sound of a helicopter in the distance. Soon it's directly overhead. A powerful searchlight comes on, and a shaft of light stabs down through the darkness, illuminating you.

Then the helicopter settles in for a landing on the end of the pier. A group of men jump out and run toward you. They are in military uniforms, except for one in civilian clothes. It's Borkin from the CIA! He comes running up to you.

Turn to page 51.

You follow the wounded student back down the road. Even though he is limping, he moves quickly.

You haven't gone far when he turns left onto a trail that winds through the mountains. It goes downward, and as you follow it, a wide valley divided by a river unfolds in front of you. Up ahead are the ruins of a washed-out bridge.

A flat raft is pulled up on the bank on your side of the river. A long pole is stuck in the ground beside it. There are fresh footprints in the muddy bank and all around the raft. Your companion is one of the few Koreans you've run into who doesn't speak any English, even a little. He gestures for you to help him push the raft into the water. Then both of you jump on board.

The Korean uses the pole to push and steer toward the other bank. As he does, the raft slowly drifts downstream.

A village of white, one-story buildings with thatched roofs and doors painted either blue or red comes into view. Rows of carved and painted posts circle the village.

As you get close to the other bank, the man ferrying you jumps off into shallow water and pulls the raft ashore. You jump out and walk through the tall grass along the river. The village is close by, and sitting in front of the houses are several bearded old men, all with immaculate white clothes and tall black stovepipe hats with narrow brims. They are smoking long bamboo pipes.

Turn to page 32.

"Ordinarily," the man says in flawless English, "new arrivals are not allowed in the hall of the Buddha. But your coming was predicted long ago. It was said that an American would appear and provide inspiration in our eternal fight against the brothers of darkness and evil. You've already survived one of their attacks."

"Do you know if Chung is all right?" you ask. "The last time I saw him, he was on the road, wounded."

"Chung is safe. He is in a village not far from where you were ambushed. When he is well enough, he will return here. He will be your instructor. My name is Choi Kyo. I am the director of the monastery. All of us here, as will you in time, serve our grand master, Kong-yi."

"Kong-yi? When will I be able to see him?" you ask.

"In time. In time you will swear complete obedience to Kong-yi, as have I and all the others here."

"Look," you say. "I just came here to study tae kwon do for the summer. I'm not really into all this other stuff."

Kyo gives a faint smile. "Well, you *came* here," he says. "That is a beginning. The rest, in time, will become clear to you."

You realize suddenly that the way things are shaping up, you might have to escape from this place at some point. For the moment, all you can do is keep your eyes and ears open and learn whatever you can.

Turn to page 41.

She goes over to her desk and picks up a small pile of gambling chips, at the same time pressing a button at the corner.

"Yun will help you place a bet," she says, handing you the chips. "Also, I will see that you are kept informed of Kenzo's condition."

Yun, the man in the tuxedo, reappears. You thank the woman and follow Yun down to the main floor.

"Humbly suggest roulette," he says, guiding you through the crowd to a central table.

"That's all right with me," you say. "I'm new at this."

"Twenty-five red most appropriate," he whispers carefully in your ear.

You follow his advice and bet your chips on that number.

The small ball spins around the roulette wheel—and comes to rest in twenty-five red!

Everyone around the table gasps, then applauds as the dealer pushes a tall pile of chips in front of you.

"Only one bet," Yun whispers. "Now good to cash."

You can barely carry all the chips as you follow him to the cashier's window. The cashier counts the chips and gives you a bank note for 20 million *won*.

Turn to page 69.

"They were lying, then," Ling says. "I am working *against* two evil men who are working within your CIA."

So much for activating the transmitter in your wristwatch.

Now that your eyes are used to the dark, you can see that Ling is wearing a black costume and face mask. Chun-chu is dressed the same way.

"You are a Ninja now?" you ask her in surprise.

"Not Ninja," Chun-chu says. "We are dressed as sul sa do fighters. It is a martial art that was first developed in Korea eighteen hundred years ago, nine hundred years before the Ninja in Japan."

"The sul sa do fighters were banished by one of the early kingdoms," Ling says. "But they took refuge in various Buddhist monasteries where they have existed underground to this day. You've heard about Kong-yi. I have joined the sul sa do to fight him. Tonight I am on a vital mission."

She turns so that you can see the large pack strapped to her back. "This contains fifty pounds of a new kind of high explosive. I'm going to plant it where it will destroy Kong-yi's operation. You can either go with me and help, or go with Chun-chu to one of the sul sa do monasteries."

You're not sure what to do—Ling helped save your life when you were in China. The least you can do is help her. On the other hand, you don't really know who Kong-yi is. Maybe it would be wrong to help destroy his operation.

If you go with Ling, turn to page 39.

If you go with Chun-chu, turn to page 105.

An hour later, Joan's limousine pulls up.

"You must leave Korea at once!" Joan exclaims. "I overheard a conversation about you in my father's office. He's involved in some kind of illegal scheme, and he wants to get you involved in it."

"What kind of scheme?"

"I wish I knew. I've tried to talk to him about it in the past, but every time I do, he sends me off to some country overseas for a year. I can't make you do anything you don't want, but here is a plane ticket back to America," she says. "We're headed for the airport at Taejon where you can get a domestic flight to Pusan, and from there a flight to the United States. My father's men are probably watching the airport near Seoul."

"Why are you doing all this for me?" you ask.

"I'll do anything if it slows my father's scheme down and saves you from being mixed up in it. I only wish I could make him see that what he's doing is wrong."

"I'll never forget your kindness," you tell Joan.

Later in the summer, you read about Joan's father in the newspapers. He was involved in a plot to overthrow the Korean government. Two unnamed employees of the American CIA are also implicated for acting against orders and aiding in the subversive plan. Somehow you know that they are Borkin and McKenna.

You hope that Joan is all right. You're glad that you left Korea when you did—you can only imagine what would have happened if you had stayed!

The End

You decide to continue on to the school.

"We go to monastery in mountains. Study tae kwon do," one of the students says in broken English.

You say good-bye to Chung and start off with three of the students. Two of them are bandaged around the head, and the third one has his arm in a sling. You follow them down to the riverbank where a small fishing boat from the village takes the four of you several miles upstream and lets you off on the other bank.

You then follow a narrow path through broad fields of wildflowers. They stretch to the foot of the mountains up ahead.

You have almost reached the mountains when you see a small puff of smoke up on the side of the first steep, wooded hill. The man next to you grabs his stomach and sinks to the ground. Then the other two students also collapse, one after the other.

You don't know what to do. You run the other way, but it doesn't do you any good. The next bullet has your name on it. Your adventure in Korea, and your brief life, are both over with one shot.

The End

You decide to escape. You scramble up the side of the hill. Kyo just stands there, his mouth hanging open. No one else seems to be coming after you.

You reach the top of a ridge, out of breath. In front of you is an endless sea of low, rolling mountain peaks.

Off to the right, not far from the cube-shaped building, you see what looks like a large door opening in the side of the mountain. A strange-looking helicopter shoots out of it and heads directly for you.

You run down the other side of the high hill, but you haven't gotten far when the flying craft hovers above you. A laser shoots down, catching you in its beam.

Your body glows for a second in an incandescent burst of light and then disintegrates into a shimmering cloud of tiny, glowing specks.

Nothing is left of you but a fine ash that settles slowly and then scatters in the breeze.

The End

"Maybe I'd better get some kind of training in before I go back to the Orient," you say.

"A wise decision," McKenna says. "Here is a rail pass. Exactly a week after your school term ends and your summer vacation begins, take the train to Springview, Maryland. You'll be met at the station and driven to the camp."

Your mother watches through the window as McKenna and Borkin walk across the lawn and get into their car. After the agents have driven away, the two of you have an argument.

"At least I can take the training," you tell your mother. "It'll be just like going to summer camp. And if I don't like it, I can just quit."

Your mother's not totally convinced, but with persistence, you win the argument.

After school closes, you pack your bag and take the train to Maryland. When you get to Springview, you get off the train and wait.

An hour later, a jeep skids to a stop next to the platform. A man in plain fatigues without any insignia leans out of the window and calls over, "Hey, kid! What's your name?"

You tell him.

"I'm here to get you," he says, reaching over and opening the door on the right side of the jeep. "Jump in. The name is McFee, General McFee," he says, putting the jeep into gear and speeding out of the station.

"General? You're a general?" you ask.

Turn to page 43.

"Your ride is paid for with flowers," the driver says. "But I would have picked you up anyway. I remember that a hundred and thirty thousand of your American people were killed or wounded defending South Korea from the North in the war. Today, many forget that."

You travel for another two hours and begin to see many modern buildings along the road.

"I'm stopping at that gas station up ahead," the driver says. "You might like to get out and stretch."

"Actually, I'd like to make a telephone call," you say. "Thanks."

You get out of the truck and go into the gas station. Fortunately, there is a pay phone there. You call the girl from the plane, Joan Pyun, at her father's office, using the number she gave you. A woman answers the phone in Korean.

"Do you speak English?" you ask.

There is a brief silence and then another voice comes on.

"Can I help you?" a man asks in English.

You explain that you are trying to get in touch with Joan Pyun.

There is another silence, a bit longer this time, then Joan answers. "Where are you?" she asks.

"Hold on a second," you say, asking one of the attendants where you are.

"I'm at a gas station in Pyong," you tell Joan.

"Stay there and I'll come and get you soon," she says and hangs up the phone.

You thank the truck driver for the lift and wave good-bye as he heads down the highway.

Turn to page 99.

You decide it's best to go with Chun-chu along the mountain trail to one of the sul sa do monasteries. About a half an hour later, the ground shakes so violently that it throws both of you to the ground.

You look back and see a thick column of flame shooting up into the air, turning the night into day. Seconds later, the earsplitting sound and the shock wave from the explosion reach you.

"I hope Ling got clear in time," Chun-chu says as you pick yourselves up and start along the trail once again.

At dawn you reach the monastery. A bell is tolling, calling the monks to meditation. A procession of them, their heads shaven, all wearing long black robes, is filing into a central building.

When the monks have all gone in, Chun-chu guides you inside. The temple is filled with candles, throwing a light that flickers off the many highly polished gold statues of the Buddha lining the inside wall.

You spend the day waiting for Ling, but she doesn't arrive.

"I fear the worst," Chun-chu says. "But I cannot allow you to leave the monastery until I have received word from her. She is the only one that can give permission."

Ling never does return to the monastery; and you never return home. Your brief trip to Korea turns out to be a very long one.

The End

Pak doesn't answer but pulls you through a door at the side of the street. "This way," he says.

You follow him through a dark hallway, and then go down a stairway to a long tunnel. Finally you come to a room with stone walls and a vaulted ceiling. A single light bulb illuminates it from high above.

"This was a bomb shelter during the war," Pak says. "We can wait here for a while."

"You and your friends at the tae kwon do school seem to have a few enemies," you say to Pak.

"That's true," he says. "I guess I have not told you everything. Of course, I didn't expect this attack. You see, we are fighting for our cause, and there are those who would stop us at any cost. I suspect that you are here for more than martial arts training."

"To tell the truth, I'm here looking for a Chinese woman named Ling. I have her picture, but I left it at the hotel."

"Ling . . . yes, I've heard of her. She's a professional assassin for the Red Dragon Society. What Chinese call Triad—gangsters, killers. They very bad."

"That can't be true," you say. "I knew her in China, and—"

You wonder if you should tell Pak about her being an agent for the CIA. Probably not. You stop yourself just in time.

"And what?" Pak asks.

Go on to the next page.

"And I just don't think she would do anything like that."

"Many good people turn bad," Pak says. "Maybe this happen to her. If you want my advice, go back home as soon as you can. If you go around asking questions about this woman Ling or about the Red Dragon Society, you won't last long in this part of the world."

Pak may have a point. So far your trip has become a little more dangerous than you expected. On the other hand, you did accept this mission and would like to keep your word. Maybe you shouldn't return home without spending at least a little more time trying to find Ling.

If you take Pak's advice and return home, turn to page 9.

If you decide to stay and keep looking for Ling, turn to page 67.

108

"I'll take the day training," you say.

"Good," McFee says. "I'll take you over to Toku's tae kwon do class."

The jeep zooms around to the other side of the buildings. There a group dressed in fatigues is doing tae kwon do exercises.

McFee motions for Toku to come over. He introduces you, then speeds away in the jeep.

"You have martial arts training already?" Toku asks.

"I've studied kung fu in China," you say.

"Maybe you can show the class what you learned there," he says.

You demonstrate some of the moves that Ling taught you.

"Very good," Toku says. "Now we start from the beginning and learn Toku techniques. Skill is all in breathing. Center of breathing is here, just below the navel. This center is the source of *chi,* or vital energy."

Turn to page 29.

You have to tell these men something. But what if you tell them about Ling? Nothing in your instructions said not to mention her. In fact, mentioning her might be a good tactic to get some information.

"All right," you say. "I'll talk. I was sent here to find a Chinese woman named Ling. I met her when I was on a kung fu tour of China last year. I haven't been able to find out anything yet because I just got here."

The man converses rapidly in Japanese with the other two men.

"Yes, you may be telling the truth," he says. "We know about this Ling woman. We'd like to find her ourselves. We know that she is somewhere in this area. Maybe not in Seoul, but operating in this part of Korea."

"You're sure?" you ask.

"As sure as—" the man starts, then looks at you angrily. "I'm the one asking the questions here!"

He says something to Moto and Matsuki, and they untie your hands and feet. You stand up uneasily.

"Don't try anything," the man says, as Moto takes out a revolver and points it at you. "And now I think you are ready for a swim in the Han River, a long swim!"

"But I told you everything," you protest.

"And you're not going to tell anyone else *anything.*"

Turn to page 46.

"I guess I'll pick night training," you say. "It sounds exciting."

"All right, then, I'll turn you over to Sergeant Dawson—as soon as it gets dark, that is. He's sleeping right now. Until then, we'll put you in sensory deprivation," McFee says.

"What is that?" you ask, sounding more than a little worried.

"It's something you'll have to get used to at night. Basically it means sitting in the dark without sounds or other stimuli."

"Like sleeping?" you ask.

"Definitely not! If you fall asleep, you're in serious trouble. Even though nothing is happening, you have to remain fully alert."

The jeep stops in front of one of the plain wooden buildings. A man comes out.

"Here is a new recruit for night training," McFee tells him. "Put him in isolation until tonight, then Sergeant Dawson will take over."

You get out of the jeep, and McFee drives off to another part of the compound. The new man then leads you into the wooden building.

"Inside here is a chamber completely enclosed by a wall several feet thick. It is made of sound-absorbing insulation," he says, opening a door to the dark inner chamber. "There is a chair in the center. Sit there, but don't get too relaxed."

He goes out and closes the door behind him, plunging you into total darkness.

Turn to page 78.

112

"I think I'll just stay in the city, at least for a while," you say.

"All right," Chung says. "Tae kwon do classes are here from ten to twelve in the morning and from eight to ten in the evening. Students are also expected to spend part of the afternoon in meditation, preferably at one of the many Buddhist temples in the city."

After you fill out the necessary papers to register for the classes, you go back to your hotel. As you enter the lobby, you notice the entrance to a fancy-looking restaurant off to one side. You decide to splurge on dinner for your first night in Seoul.

The headwaiter seats you at one of the smaller tables near the window. Outside you can see the television tower atop the high hill behind the hotel. The lights of a cable car shuttle up and down the steep hillside.

The restaurant has two menus, a typical American one featuring steak and potatoes, and one in Korean. This lists various kinds of *kimchi,* which must be the Korean national dish. There is a note at the bottom of the menu warning foreign visitors that kimchi is basically a mixture of vegetables and hot peppers, and that it is *very* spicy. You decide to try at least a taste of it.

You order and then sit back to enjoy the view while you are waiting. As you do, a familiar reflection appears in the window glass. You turn to see Joan Pyun standing there. She is smiling.

Turn to page 19.

After the van stops in front of the castle, the men escort you inside. You find yourself in a garden, complete with a pond, large, weathered rocks, and a miniature waterfall. All of this is in an inner court-yard. A small teahouse is on the other side of the pond.

"Take off shoes, please," one of the men says as he bows and slides open the paper-covered lat-ticed door to the teahouse. You have to duck down to enter.

Inside you see a man, his head shaved like a monk, dressed in a dark green kimono. He is kneeling in front of a brazier.

"Sit here," he says, handing you a cup of tea. "I want to talk to you about your reasons for being here. This Ling whom your CIA seeks so desper-ately is a problem for us as well. Our problem is, we don't know whether to believe her or not. She says that we should make peace with the Chinese Triads, criminal organizations that are in competi-tion with our own illegal traffic. She says that a Korean gangster named Kong-yi would like the Yakuza and Triads to have a gang war in which we would wipe each other out. Then he would pick up the pieces. We need you to find out from Ling if this is really true."

Turn to page 90.

"Singapore sounds good," you say.

"I'll arrange for your flight to Singapore International Airport right away," McFee says. "Before you leave you will be given special dark glasses that will protect your eyes during the day. Your cover will be that you are blind—hoping for a miraculous cure at the Buddhist shrine on Belau, a small island near the much larger island of Singapore itself. Once there, your local CIA contact will meet you at the shrine."

You land at the airport a day later. You are assisted through customs, and a cab takes you to a small motorboat ferry on the waterfront for your trip to the island of Belau.

Halfway there, you are grabbed from behind—with your dark glasses on, you can't see by whom. Whoever they are, they yank your money and passport from your pockets and push you overboard.

As you tread water, you watch the boat speed away. Fortunately, there is a small island nearby. You swim ashore and walk up the broad, sparkling white beach to a village.

The people there are friendly and don't mind that you have no money or identification, even that you don't speak their language. The beach turns out to be great for surfing.

You decide to wait for a while before you inform the CIA where you are.

The End

116

"I'll go to Korea to search for Ling," you tell McFee.

A flight has been reserved for you on a commercial airline. A truck soon arrives and takes you to Dulles International Airport near Washington, DC. Agents Borkin and McKenna are there to see you off.

When you land near Seoul, South Korea, a CIA operative meets you at the airport and drives you to the city itself. He helps you check into the Hilton hotel and wishes you good luck before leaving.

Turn to page 42.

You jump up from the table and dash after Kenzo, following him. Just before you go through the door of the kitchen, you see the three men running in your direction. Inside, Kenzo makes a flying leap over a long kitchen table and, without breaking stride, bounds up a stairway on the other side.

You are going too fast to stop and crash into the kitchen table—scattering pots and pans in all directions. You slide across the table and fall to the floor. By the time you pick yourself up, the three men are coming through the door. You grab the handle of a large pot of hot soup on the stove next to you and splatter it in their direction. It catches two of them in the face, and they stop chasing you, falling to the floor in pain. The third man is almost on top of you as you reach the stairway. He grabs you by your foot. You kick with your other foot as hard as you can, catching him in the knee. He lets go and tumbles backward.

You run up the stairway after Kenzo, but he has disappeared. At the top is a door to the street. As you come out, you bump into two more goons.

When you wake up, you are in a hospital. Borkin and McKenna and a nurse are leaning over you, looking at you anxiously.

"When you get out of the hospital, we've arranged for you to spend a couple of weeks resting on the beach in Hawaii," McKenna says. "Then we hope you will rejoin our team here in Korea. Of course, we'll leave the decision up to you."

"I'll think about it," you say. But secretly, you doubt it.

The End

"I remember Macao," you say. "I was there when I was in China. It might be interesting."

"A special plane with a darkroom will fly you to Hong Kong. Once there, at night of course, you will be transferred to a small seaplane and put down on the South China Sea off the coast of Macao," McFee says. "The main headquarters of the Red Dragon Society is in an old Portuguese villa on a high bluff overlooking the sea. We have reason to believe that Ling may be staying there."

An hour after sunset the following day, you are on a rubber raft close to the beach off Macao. The lights of the villa are at the top of a high cliff directly ahead. You beach the raft next to some large rocks and start climbing upward. You have no trouble finding your way—you can now see in almost total darkness.

Just before you get to the top of the cliff, all the lights in the villa go out. At the top, you flatten yourself against the building and work your way toward a dark window. You are peering through when the lights come back on.

The burst of light temporarily blinds you—you've been in darkness for so long. An ordinary light bulb now seems as bright as the sun.

Before your eyes can adjust to the light, several hands grab you and heave you back over the cliff.

You still can't see anything during the long fall, nor do you feel anything when you finally hit the rocks at the bottom.

The End

You slip out of bed, feel around for your clothing, and get dressed. Then you follow the monk outside.

Even though it's a summer night, a cool breeze is blowing down from the mountains. There is no moon, but the stars are scattered throughout the sky, providing just enough light for you to see by.

The silhouette of the monk is moving across the courtyard. You can see that he is gesturing for you to follow.

There is an open gate at the far side. You follow him through it and move away from the walls.

You catch up with him about thirty yards away in a grove of trees.

"We can talk now—but not too loud," he says. "My name is Chun-chu. Ling will meet us at the ridge."

"Ling? Really?"

"She is just as surprised that *you* are here," Chun-chu says.

You follow him upward along a narrow trail. The valley behind you is a pool of darkness, but the large, cube-shaped building on the side of the mountain seems to glow.

At the top of the trail, you see a dark shadow moving among the rocks.

You don't realize who it is until she speaks.

"It is good to see you again," Ling says. "At least what I can see of you in the dark."

"Ling!" you say. "It's really you. I was sent here to find you by two CIA agents. They said you were one of them and you were missing."

Turn to page 98.

ABOUT THE AUTHOR

RICHARD BRIGHTFIELD is a graduate of Johns Hopkins University, where he studied biology, psychology, and archaeology. For many years he worked as a graphic designer at Columbia University. He has written many books in the Choose Your Own Adventure series, including *Planet of the Dragons, Hurricane!,* and *Master of Kung Fu.* In addition, Mr. Brightfield has coauthored more than a dozen game books with his wife, Glory. The Brightfields and their daughter, Savitri, live in Gardiner, New York.

ABOUT THE ILLUSTRATOR

FRANK BOLLE studied at Pratt Institute. He has worked as an illustrator for many national magazines and now creates and draws cartoons for magazines as well. He has also worked in advertising and children's educational materials and has drawn and collaborated on several newspaper comic strips, including *Annie* and *Winnie Winkle.* Most recently he has illustrated *Master of Kung Fu, South Pole Sabotage, Return of the Ninja, You Are A Genius, Through the Black Hole,* and *The Worst Day of Your Life* in the Choose Your Own Adventure series. A native of Brooklyn Heights, New York, Mr. Bolle now lives and works in Westport, Connecticut.